This book belongs to:

Contents

Ladybird

Cover illustration by Rosslyn Moran

A catalogue record for this book is available from the British Library

Published by Ladybird Books Ltd
A subsidiary of the Penguin Group
A Pearson Company

Now it's your turn

written by Marie Birkinshaw
illustrated by Rosslyn Moran

It was our school Sports Day.

All the mums and dads had come to watch.

The green team went first.
They ran over the jumps,
under the nets and...

crash!

out went the Greens.

The mums and dads
tried hard not to laugh.

The blue team shouted,
"Now it's our turn."
And off they ran. They went
over the jumps, under the nets,
round the track and...

smash!

out went the Blues.

This time the mums and dads couldn't stop laughing.

"It must be our turn by now,"
shouted the yellow team.
They were the favourites to win.
They ran over the jumps, under
the nets, round the track, along
the wall and...

splash!

out went the Yellows.

The mums and dads were really laughing now.

"Well," said Mrs Brown, the Head Teacher. "Someone will have to win." She looked at all the mums and dads.

"So now it's **your** turn!"

The mums and dads went over the fence, through the playground and ran away to their cars.

And this time **we** had a really good laugh.

The other side

written by Marie Birkinshaw
illustrated by Tania Hurt-Newton

They have Angry Anna
and Tiger Tim.
They have Pushy Pete
and Crashing Kim.
They have Matthew Mad
and Gary Grim.
We really don't like
the look of him.

They have Bouncer Ben
and Fighter Fred.
They have Lucky Lucy
and Noisy Ned.
They have Jumping James
and Giant Jed.

But they won't get the ball
round our Tiny Ted!

The school report

written by Lorraine Horsley
illustrated by Peta Blackwell

Mum came to collect me from school.

She could see that I was worried about my school report.

She took the envelope from me and put it in her bag.

When we got home, I went up to my room.

I thought she would be angry when she read the report.

I heard her come upstairs.

"Come on, David," Mum said.
"Your dinner's getting cold!"

"It's your favourite,
chips and beans."

I said I wasn't hungry.

"Are you all right?" she asked.

"Yes," I said quietly, and she went downstairs.

Dad came home from work.

I heard him shout up the stairs, “David, come down here, please!”

I walked very, very slowly
into the kitchen. I saw the
open envelope on the table.

"Here, read your school report,"
Dad said.

I looked at the report.
This is what it said.

School Report

MATHS	Very good work.
READING	David's reading is coming along very well.
SPELLING	Excellent.
SCIENCE	David likes Science. He works very hard.
SPORTS	David is the best runner in the class.

David is very helpful in class and always tries his best. Well done.

I wasn't worried any more.

"Can I have my beans and chips now, please, Mum?"

Winding words

written by Shirley Jackson
illustrated by Justin Grassi

Read this line and you will find that round and round the words will wind. Read again and you will see that all the words wind round to me.

Winding words

Have fun following the words as they wind round towards the centre of the maze. Your child will enjoy seeing reading text presented in an unusual way.

New words

Encourage your child to use some of these new words to write his own very simple stories and rhymes.

Read with Ladybird...

is specially designed to help your child learn to read. It will complement all the methods used in schools.

Parents took part in extensive research to ensure that **Read with Ladybird** would help your child to:

- take the first steps in reading
- improve early reading progress
- gain confidence in new-found abilities.

The research highlighted that the most important qualities in helping children to read were that:

- books should be fun – children have enough 'hard work' at school
- books should be colourful and exciting
- stories should be up to date and about everyday experiences
- repetition and rhyme are especially important in boosting a child's reading ability.

The stories and rhymes introduce the 100 words most frequently used in reading and writing.

These 100 key words actually make up half the words we use in speech and reading.

The three levels of **Read with Ladybird** consist of 22 books, taking your child from two words per page to 600-word stories.

Read with Ladybird will help your child to master the basic reading skills so vital in everyday life.

Ladybird have successfully published reading schemes and programmes for the last 50 years. Using this experience and the latest research, **Read with Ladybird** has been produced to give all children the head start they deserve.

Level 1 – Start reading

For a child who is at the first reading stage – whether he or she is at school or about to start school. Uses rhyme and repetitive phrases to build sentences and introduces and emphasises important words relating to everyday childhood experiences.

Level 2 – Improve reading

Building on the reading skills taught at home and in school, this level helps your child to practise the first 100 key words. The stories help develop your child's interest in reading with structured texts while maintaining the fun of learning to read.

Level 3 – Practise reading

At this level, your child is able to practise new-found skills and move from reading out loud to independent silent reading. The longer stories and rhymes develop reading stamina and introduce different styles of writing and a variety of subjects. At the end of this level your child will have read around 1000 different words.

Learning to read with this book

Now it's your turn

Show how much you enjoy listening as your child reads this story to you. If he hesitates at any of the words, wait for a few seconds to see if he can work the word out or correct himself. If not, give the word or the sound at the beginning of the word, and encourage him to re-read that sentence and then carry on.
Encourage him to read the story again either straightaway or perhaps the next day.

The other side

Offer to help your child with the names in this rhyme and then encourage him to read it fluently, with lots of fun and acting out!

The school report

When your child has read this story to you, talk about what happened. How does David feel? What does your child think of David's report?